James Relly

Thoughts on the cherubimical mystery

An attempt to prove, that the Cherubims were emblems of salvation, by the blood

of Jesus.

James Relly

Thoughts on the cherubimical mystery
An attempt to prove, that the Cherubims were emblems of salvation, by the blood of Jesus.

ISBN/EAN: 9783741198793

Manufactured in Europe, USA, Canada, Australia, Japa

Cover: Foto ©Andreas Hilbeck / pixelio.de

Manufactured and distributed by brebook publishing software (www.brebook.com)

James Relly

Thoughts on the cherubimical mystery

ON THE

CHERUBIMICAL MYSTERY;

Or an ATTEMPT to prove,

That the CHERUBIMS were EMBLEMS
of SALVATION,

By the BLOOD of JESUS.

---

*Whom he hath appointed heir of all things: by whom also
he made the worlds.* Heb. i. 2.

He is before all things, and by him all things consist.

By JAMES RELLY.

LONDON:
Printed in the Year M.DCC.LXXX.

THOUGHTS

ON THE

Cherubimical Myſtery, &c.

THE firſt mention made of cherubims, in the ſacred writings, is in *Gen.* iii. 24. when, upon *Adam*'s being diveſted of dominion, and driven out of the garden of *Eden*, for breach of covenant, the cherubims were placed at the end of the garden, to prevent his return thither.

The next mention we have of cherubims, is in *Exod.* xxv. 18. where God commanded *Moſes* to make two cherubims of beaten gold, in the ends of the mercy-ſeat; and ſo to adjuſt them, that, covering the mercy-ſeat with their wings, and having their faces turned the one to the other, they might both be looking towards the mercy-ſeat. *Solomon* is alſo ſaid to have made cherubims of olive-tree; and, overlaying them with gold, to have placed them in the inner houſe, even in the ſacred oracle: the doors and walls of which houſe round about, were alſo ornamented with cherubims carved upon them.

But

But yet, the defcription of the cherubims, refpecting their figure, is very obfcure, until we come to the prophet *Ezekiel*'s account of them, who tells us, " They had the likenefs of a " man : each of them had four faces; the face " of a man, and the face of a lion, on the right " fide, and the face of an ox, on the left fide; " they alfo each of them had the face of an " eagle. They had ftraight feet, and the fole " of them was like the fole of a calve's foot, " and they fparkled like the colour of burnifh- " ed brafs. They each of them had four " wings, and under their wings they had the " hands of a man, on their four fides."— After this manner the prophet defcribes them ; nor is the variation or difference between this and *John's* account of them *(Rev.* iv.) at all material. The apoftle, indeed, calls them beafts; fo the prophet had called them crea- tures. The apoftle fays, they were four, and that they were in the midft of the throne, and round about the throne, and that they were full of eyes before and behind. The firft beaft was like a lion, the fecond like a calf, and the third had the face as a man, and the fourth was like a flying eagle : and the four had each of them fix wings about him : and they were full of eyes within, and they reft not day nor night, faying, holy, holy, holy Lord God Almighty ! which was, and is, and is to come.

From

From thefe defcriptions, I propofe to attempt
an explication of the Cherubimical Myftery:
by fhewing, The origin of the cherubim, and
the medium of their appearance.—The reafon
and fpirit of their figure; and their connection
with the wheels, as feen in the prophet's vifion;
with a view to a proper evangelical ufe of the
doctrine.

" And I looked (faith the prophet) and be-
" hold, a whirlwind came out of the north, a
" great cloud, and a fire infolding itfelf, and a
" brightnefs was about it, and out of the midft
" thereof as the colour of amber, out of the
" midft of the fire. Alfo, out of the midft
" thereof came the likenefs of four living crea-
" tures, and this was their appearance, they
" had the likenefs of a man, &c."—In the
fides of the north is fituated the city of the
great king —The title of the great king was
given by the ancient *Greeks* to the *Perfian* mo-
narch, as the moft powerful of their neigh-
bours: and even, before this æra, we find the
king of *Affyria* affuming the title of great king.
But the *Hebrew* nation, who were inftructed
not to give flattering titles to men, conftantly
applied the title of *Great King* to the Lord
their God.

The city of the great king, as fituated in the
fides of the north, is generally applied (I think)
to the literal *Jerufalem*; and the 14th chapter
of *Ifaiah* is expounded fo as to ferve this purpofe.—The *Lucifer*, fon of the morning, there
de-

defcribed, as faying in his heart, " I will
" afcend into heaven ; I will exalt my throne
" above the ftars of God ; I will fit alfo upon
" the mount of the congregation, in the fides
" of the north."— This *Lucifer* (I fay) is
commonly fuppofed to be the king of *Babylon*.

But this hypothefis is liable to more objec-
tions than one : it is an error in geography to
make *Jerufalem* north of *Babylon*; the reverfe
being true. It does not appear to have been
the defign of the king of *Babylon*, at any time,
to fix his throne at *Jerufalem*; nay, when he
led his armies againft her, it was rather with a
view to diveft her of power, to raze her foun-
dations, and to lay her glory in the duft, than
to make her the houfe of his kingdom, or the
place his throne fhould be eftablifhed.

Hence, the reafon and fpirit of the 14th of
Ifaiah, muft be looked for elfewhere, than in
any thing applicable to the literal *Jerufalem*,
and to the king of *Babylon*. But, by fuch
who are attached to the letter, and who never
go any further in their enquiries after truth, it
will be here urged, that the Pfalmift intends
the literal *Jerufalem* ; where he fays, " Beau-
" tiful for fituation, the joy of the whole earth,
" is Mount *Zion* ; on the fides of the north is
" the city of the great king."— If this be applied to the *Jerufalem* which is above, who is
free with her children, and who is the mother
of us all, it is indeed juft and glorious. But it
may

may not, with propriety, bear a literal applica-
tion: for, refpecting the *Jerufalem* which was
below, and which was ever in bondage with
her children, it does not appear that fhe excel-
led in the beauty of her fituation, nor that fhe
was the joy of the whole earth; nor that fhe
ftood in the fides of the north; nor that any
prince who ever governed in her was ftiled the
great king: for where fhe is at any time, by
way of eminence or diftinction, called the city
of God, the holy city, &c. it is only in a typical fenfe that fhe is thus called, as fhe was a
figure of the perfect church, the fpiritual *Jerufalem*: for, literally, fhe hath very different
characters in the fcriptures. — I come now to
propofe, that the north, in the fides of which
is the city of the great king, and the north
from whence the cherubims originated, is rather
to be underftood allegorically than otherwife:
it refpects the nature and perfon of man.—For
God being to the whole creation of intelligent
beings, both celeftial and terreftrial, what the
fun, as a figure, is to the latter; thofe beings
may be denominated north, fouth, &c. juft as
they, from their dignity of nature, or ftation,
may be fituated more or lefs in the fhine of
divine favour, and in the enjoyment of the
glory of God.

Of thofe beings, the angels excel in dignity
and ftrength; abound moft in power and glory;
and dwelling more immediately *in*, and enjoy-

ing

ing more abundantly the prefence of God, they have *among them*, as the chambers of the fouth, perpetual warmth, verdure, and fruitfulnefs.

But man, being originally from nature and fta-tion, lower than the angels, and more remote from the views and enjoyments of the brightnefs and glory of God, is as the colder north, lefs warm, lefs fruitful, lefs verdant: and yet, fuch is the will of the Almighty, fuch the riches of our Creator's love towards us, that he hath made choice of the fides of the barren north for his habitation; there to raife the mount of the congregation, there to build the city of the great King! and this he effected, by taking on him not the nature of angels, but the feed of *Abraham.*

Man, from his firft creation, being confider-ed as the north, it is not unnatural to fuppofe, that the whirlwind, which the prophet faw coming from thence, intended man's fall and rebellion againft God, which was fudden and rapid as the whirlwind. Whirlwinds are often faid to come out of the fouth, which the fcrip-tures reprefent as according to nature: but, except in the prophet's vifion of the cherubim, I remember not to have read of a whirlwind coming out of the north. Hence, the account is ufhered in with a note of attention and wonder; BEHOLD, a whirlwind came out of the NORTH! &c. This is, at leaft, an intima-tion that it related to fomething extremely rare

and

and fingular, the repetition of which was not to be expected. Nor is there any thing fo fully pointed out by fuch a figure, as is the great tranfgreffion, which man having once committed, hath it not in his power to commit again.

The great cloud may intend that dark and clouded ftate wherein the human foul was involved upon its departure from God, and which rendered all the profpects and expectations of man unfpeakably gloomy and dreadful.

The fire infolding itfelf, denotes guilt, the natural fruit of iniquity, and which the fcriptures compare to fire; whilft the brightnefs round about, may imply conviction; confifting of remembrance, reflection, and confcioufnefs, and aptly confidered as a brightnefs diftinct from the fire.

The colour of amber fhining out of the midft of the fire, is not without its fignificancy. The origin of amber hath been controverted, whilft, refpecting its qualities, as more demonftrable, there is a general agreement.

That amber is originally liquid, may, as I think, be gathered from its containing flies and other infects, which, upon its being broken, may be difcerned in its moft folid parts. That which is gathered from the fea, may probably be confolidated, partly by the falts, and partly by the fermentation and friction of the waves: hence it is emblematical of punifhment for fin,

B   which

which receives its force from the tumultuous diftreffes of the guilty mind. The wicked are compared to the troubled fea, whofe waters cannot reft.

Amber, is an inflammable fubftance, and greatly bituminous, and is in this a figure of the punifhment due to fin, which, in the fcriptures, is reprefented under the fimilitude of fire, burning pitch, and brimftone.

Amber, is alfo of note for its electrical powers, another figure of the punifhment of fin, which punifhment being juft and equitable, draws into its vortex, for chaftifement and annihilation, every evil work, word, and thought.

The natural colour of amber is a pale yellow; and the prophet feeing this colour in the midft of the fire, it denoted that guilt hath its punifhment in itfelf, and yet each diftinguifhable from the other.

Upon the above hypothefis I raife this propofition, The whirlwind coming out of the north, with the cloud of fire, &c. were emblematical of the fall, with all its dreadful confequences; conviction, guilt, gloom, horror, defpair, death and hell, as the punifhment thereof.

Out of the midft of this appearance the prophet faw the likenefs of four living creatures come forth, " and this was their appear- " ance, they had the likenefs of a man."— The cherubims had, indeed, their origin from
the

the Father of Lights : but the medium of their manifeſtation, and the only given reaſon of their utility, was from the fall of man, unto which they owe their appearance, uſefulneſs, and indeed the apparent reaſon of their exiſtence; God having purpoſed in himſelf to glorify the riches of his grace by thoſe means.—We read nothing of the cherubims until after *Adam*'s tranſgreſſion : for, though they exiſted with God before (unto whom were known all his works from the foundation of the world) yet the reaſon and time of their appearance were not come until fin entered; but then they were immediately appointed to guard the way of the tree of life.

As I expect it will not be controverted, that the cherubims or living creatures, which the prophet faw, are the ſame with thoſe which *John* beheld in his viſion, mentioned before, I ſhall, firſt, conſider the deſcription according to the latter, and that, as I judge, will throw ſome light upon the former.

John ſays, " That the firſt was like a lion, " the ſecond like a calf, the third had a face " as a man, and the fourth was like a flying " eagle : each had ſix wings, and were full " of eyes : and they reſt not day nor night " from ſaying, holy, holy, holy Lord God " Almighty ! which was, and is, and is to " come."

B 2   This

This I would explain as follows—The number four intends the four principal particulars of redemption by our Lord Jesus Christ—The face of a man denotes Christ's incarnation, or the Word made flesh—The face of the calf, ox, or heifer, was significant of his sacrifice— The lion, ever victorious, is prince of the foreft, and, at his roar, the whole nation of beafts tremble : this likenefs is manifeftly the fymbol of power, and implies our Lord's refurrection, when he gave proof of his having trodden down ftrength, of his having fubdued and deftroyed fin, and hell, and death, with him who had the power of death, even the devil. The refurrection of Jefus had power to unbind, juftify and difcharge from all fin, the helplefs fons of men : yea, at his refurrection, he had all power in heaven and in earth given into his hand, and therefore fitly reprefented by the lion.

The eagle, from the ftrength of its pinion, foaring above the reach of human eye, and from its piercing fight, has always been confidered hieroglyphical of the fublime, the exalted, and the glorious, and therefore beautifully points out our blefled Lord's afcenfion.—Thus thefe four faces, in their myftic defign, bear witnefs to the great falvation.

Their being full of eyes before and behind, fhews the redemption of our Lord Jefus Chrift
look-

looking backward to *Adam*, and forward to his offspring, even to the end of time.

Their wings intend the divine attributes; mercy, truth, righteoufnefs, peace, wifdom and love; upon the confent and harmony of which the Redeemer and his Redemption afcend above all heavens.

Ezekiel faw but four wings to the cherubim, becaufe the rich difplay of divine wifdom and love, in the redemption of mankind, was re-ferved for the New Teftament ftate, the heights and depths of which were manifefted to the apoftles, and hence it was that *John* faw fix wings.

The prophet difcovered under the wings of the cherubim the hands of a man, which im-plies that authority and qualification derived to the Saviour from the harmony of the divine attributes in his great and finifhed falvation.—— From whence, as the reward of his toils, he merited and was qualified to receive gifts for men, even the rebellious, that the Lord their God might dwell among them.—From hence, alfo, he has obtained that all power in heaven and in earth fhould be put into his hands.

It is faid of thofe which *John* faw, that they were full of eyes within, which denotes inward light and confcious purity. As all human righteoufneffes are compared to fepulchres, which, though they be beautified and whiten-ed without, are within full of rottennefs, filth,

and

and darknefs, fo in contradiftinction to the righteoufnefs of man.—The righteoufnefs of our Lord Jefus Chrift is reprefented, in the beauties of holinefs, as full of eyes within: for, when he undertook the caufe of man, and yet to vindicate the ways of God with him, he drew not his bow at a venture, but purfued his plan in fure and certain hope, confcious of the equity and righteoufnefs of his proceedings and fuccefs; every face of his falvation was full of eyes within, light, life, health and purity.

It is alfo faid of thofe which *John* faw, that they reft not day nor night, but inceffantly cry, holy, holy, holy, &c.—This fhews, that the redemption of mankind by our Lord Jefus Chrift (that glorious work and labour of love!) is the fource of everlafting praife unto God and to the Lamb.—All his works praife him, but peculiarly that work of wifdom and love where he hath faved us, and called us with an holy calling; not according to works of righteoufnefs as wrought by us, but according to his own purpofe and grace, given us in Jefus Chrift, before the world began. From this grace the Almighty receives the moft fpiritual and continual praife.—This bleffed grace can afcribe unto the Father of Lights, not only wifdom, mercy, and love, but holinefs, and that in perfect harmony, and confiftent with his

infinite

infinite perfections: hence the perpetual cry of holy, holy, holy.

It was upon this glory given to God, and not before, that the four-and-twenty elders fell down before him that fat on the throne, and worfhipped him that liveth for ever, and ever, cafting their crowns before his throne, faying, " Thou art worthy, O Lord, to receive glory " and honour and power; for thou haft crea- " ted all things, and for thy pleafure they are " and were created."

From the above we are taught, That the elders have their matter, fpirit, and right of praife, from the great redemption.—When the faces of falvation, in truth and juftice, afcribe holinefs to God, and rejoice in his purity thereby, preaching the everlafting gofpel, and giving proof to man of the harmony of the divine properties in Jefus Chrift, by whom all things confift, then it is that all thofe who re- joice in that falvation, fhout forth the praifes of the Lord, and beings taught to know him, who was from the beginning, they learn the end and defign of their creation.

From the remarks which I have already made, I truft it will be feen that *John*'s de- fcription of the beafts, is exactly coincident with *Ezekiel*'s defcription of the cherubim; both containing, in my judgment, the fame myftery, without any material difference in the defcription.

I have

I have already hinted, that though the faces of falvation were ever before the divine prefence, God having from everlafting appointed us to falvation by Jefus Chrift, yet it was by means of the fall of man that the divine decree, refpecting this matter, was revealed to him.—Though the grace and glory of our Lord Jefus Chrift, comprehended in the Cherubimical Myftery, was the eternal delight of the Moft·High, and what he had as the firft and principal in view when he made the worlds.—Yet, until the fall, neither the excellence nor neceffity of this grace appeared.

Thus we may confider the cherubims coming out of the whirlwind, the cloud, the fire, &c. to be the revelation of Chrift, refpecting the method and glory of his falvation, manifefting itfelf by means of the fall : then mankind had the firft fpecimen of God's wonderful working, where, out of the eater, he brought meat, and out of the ftrong, fweetnefs; and, without controverfy, taught us that all things work together for our good.

The cherubims, as fymbols of falvation by Jefus Chrift, were placed at the eaft end of the garden of *Eden*, accompanied by a flaming fword which turned every way to defend the way of the tree of life : but of this I fhall have occafion to fpeak hereafter.

All things, man in particular, being made for Jefus Chrift, defigned as an inheritance for

a be-a beloved fon, fubjects for a prince, a flock for the fhepherd, and a bride for the bridegroom, they were deftined to a ftate of eternal dependance on him. Man being originally formed for the glory of Chrift, his firft creation ftate, refpecting righteoufnefs and holinefs, was fimply figurative. Hence the apoftle tells us, that *Adam* was a figure of him that was to come.

Adam, while he lived in the figure only, knew not the intent of his exiftence, nor that there was before him a greater good than he yet enjoyed. Naturally fuppofing that his innocence entitled him to the favour of God, he muft neceffarily conclude, that his continuance in the ftate of innocence would fecure to him that favour. This idea originated in *Adam* from the entrance of the law, notwithftanding it entered for other purpofes; and though it was immediately fuperfeded by the gofpel, in the promife of the woman's feed, to bruife the ferpent's head, yet the taint remains, the prejudice is confpicuous in his offspring, who generally fay, that if *Adam* had obferved the precept, he and his pofterity would have been faved by his obedience : and that *Adam*, being a free agent, inftead of tranfgreffing as he did, might have continued in his righteoufnefs, and thereby fecured eternal life to himfelf and to his offspring.

But this, in my judgment, is fuch an egregious miftake, as betrays an abfolute ignorance

C   of

of the fcriptures, and of the power of God.—
The apoftle fays, " If there had been a law
" given which could have given life, verily
" righteoufnefs fhould have been by the law,"
Gal. iii. 21.—Hence I argue, the infufficiency
of the law given to *Adam*, to give him life,
was becaufe it had no fuch appointment: it
was not given him for that end, as appears
from *Rom.* v. 20. " Moreover, the law entered
" that the offence might abound."—From hence
it may be inferred, that *Adam*'s obedience, had
he perfifted in it, would not have intitled him
to eternal life: forafmuch as the falvation of
Jefus was not an incidental affair, dependant on
contingencies, but a matter fixed in the fore-
knowledge, and by the determinate counfel of
God, who had not appointed us, unto wrath,
but to obtain falvation by our Lord Jefus Chrift:
nor was it poffible that any effort of the creature fhould fruftrate this decree of the Creator;
therefore he could at no time obtain falvation
by the works of his own hands.

Human wifdom hath feigned, and tradition
keeps it in countenance, that God promifed falvation to *Adam* on condition of his obedience:
but this is not the doctrine of the fcriptures;
nay, from thefe the contrary is manifeft, as appears from obfervations already made.

Nor does it follow, becaufe *Adam* was threat-
ened with death on the day he eat of the for-
bidden fruit, that he was to inherit eternal life

on

on condition of his abſtinence: this being, at beſt, but negative holineſs; and, with the nature of things, inconſiſtently entitled to reward. Moreover, the apoſtle aſſures us, that the promiſe was not through the law.

As to the pretence that *Adam* had a freedom of will, and that the choice of good or evil was in his power; I reply, the power, or even the poſſibility of chooſing evil, is incompatible with a perfect ſtate. Hence I infer, that *Adam*, as a perfect man, could have no diſpoſition to chooſe the evil.

If it depended on the creature's choice whether he would be ſaved by his own righteouſneſs or not, then was it in the creature's power to confirm or diſannul the decrees of his Creator; than which to imagine, there can be nothing (in my judgment) more abſurd and impious.

To ſuppoſe the ſame perſon having an equal freedom of choice towards good and evil, is an abſurdity much more glaring than that of a hermaphrodite in the human kind. It is a creature in equilibrio, between good and evil, and yet not ſo, becauſe he choſe the evil rather than the good: theſe and many more are the inconſiſtencies deducible from the notion of free-agency in man.

I am aware of what will be deemed a full anſwer to this, *i. e.* "The balance in man had "not inclined to evil but for the interpoſition

C 2 " of

" of an enemy."—To which I anfwer, a fort, defcribed as above, could not be taken but from a traitor within, or from the will of the prince to difmantle and give it up.—I am confirmed in this from a faying of our Saviour's : " For " the prince of this world cometh, and hath " nothing in me."—Jefus being a perfect man, had not the evil feed in him, and therefore when tempted was not overcome.—*Adam*, originally, had not the evil feed in him, and therefore could not have been overcome by temptation : nor can the fubtilty nor force of the enemy effect any thing againft perfection.

The caufe, therefore, of the lapfe muft be fought for elfewhere, and the Pfalmift explains it as follows : " Thou turneft man to deftruc- " tion."—As the hufbandman turns his vineyard to deftruction, by neglecting its fences and culture ; fo that, inftead of the vine and the fig-tree, thorns and thiftles over-run it ; and the wild boar of the wood having accefs, uproots every pleafant plant.

The apoftle fays, " The creature was made " fubject to vanity, not willingly, but by rea- " fon of him who fubjected the fame in hope," *Rom.* viii. 20. That *Adam* was the creature here intended, will not (as I fuppofe) be queftioned : and in that he was MADE fubject to vanity, it implies that he did not fubject himfelf to it.—He was *made* fubject not willingly— This muft intend either the will of him who

made

made the creature fubject, or the will of the creature himfelf; but the firft cannot be intended, whether the power who fubjected the creature be fuppofed to be gracious or malignant.

I am aware of the common received opinion, that it was fatan who fubjected the creature to vanity; but, furely, it cannot be faid of him that he acted unwillingly in the affair.—Nor can it be faid of the Almighty, where he is fuppofed to have fubjected the creature to vanity, that he did it unwillingly, as it would imply him under a neceffity of acting contrary to his will: it muft therefore intend the will of the *creature himfelf*.—From thence I infer, that the will of the *creature* was not concerned in his fubjection, nor was it the confequence of his choice, for that would neceffarily imply that the creature had, from creation, an evil bias, which confifts not with the purity of the Creator.

But the creature was made fubject to vanity by reafon of him who fubjected the fame in hope; *i. e.* as I humbly conceive, by reafon of Jefus Chrift, who being originally appointed heir of ALL things, ALL things, MAN in particular, being made for him, thefe were the appointed means by which he was to gain poffeffion of his own.—As the figure muft neceffarily give place to the fubftance, it was requifite that the creature fhould be fubjected to vanity,

nity, that the purpofe and grace given him in Chrift Jefus, before the world began, might take that place unto which it was appointed.

If the Saviour is the perfon by reafon of whom the creature was fubjected to vanity, the inference is eafy refpecting that will and power which fubjected him, though done by the agency of him, who acting as an enemy, nor fought nor expected ought lefs than the ruin of the creature. That the ferpent, or fatan, did it, is what the fcriptures affirm, but the will of God limits the power of fatan, and the wifdom of God over-rules all his devices; fo that fatan's doing it, is no denial of his doing it by the determinate will of God, and by reafon of Chrift. The fubtilty and enmity of the ferpent to God and Man being made, in this particular, to fubferve the purpofe of grace. Thus Chrift appointing, over-ruling, and conducting, may be confidered as the power, by reafon of whom, and by whom, the creature was fubjected to vanity in hope, though effected by the agency of another.—— I am aware that fundry affect to make wide diftinctions between appointment and permiffion, and, as they relate to man, fuch diftinctions may be juft; but, furely, when applied to the Divine Being, they are unwarrantable, yea abfolutely wrong.

Man, defective in knowledge, fore-knowledge, in wifdom and power, may permit what he does not appoint; yea, what may be contrary to his choice, becaufe (by him) not to be prevented.

But fuch diftinctions are by no means applicable to him who is in himfelf the fulnefs of all perfection. However men philofophize, or play the fophift, it is impoffible, to common fenfe, to feparate neceffity from fore-knowledge. God foreknew that *Adam* would fall; but it was impoffible for infinite wifdom to be miftaken, *Adam* muft fall, nor was it in himfelf to prevent it. All power is of God; therefore whatfoever *is* to the fore-knowledge of God, is fo in confequence of his own appointment. Fore-knowledge may be confidered as the confcioufnefs which the Divine Being has of his decrees, they being infallible, not to be fruftrated nor altered, and therefore, with all their fruits and confequences ever before him, irreverfible and unavoidable. Nor doth he permit but what tends to fulfil his decrees. Hence, all affectations to diftinguifh between the decree and the permiffion, in God, have more fubtilty than fimplicity, as expedients contrived by the wifdom of this world to exculpate the Almighty from the charge of acting inconfiftent to the rules which human prudence dictates to him. But common fenfe fays, what God permits he foreknew, and what he foreknew he had decreed.

I have obferved, that Chrift was the perfon by reafon of whom, or on whofe account, the creature was made fubject to vanity; and that notwithftanding it was done by fatan, yet he being made to ferve the glory of Chrift in that particular, and employed to fulfil the decree, the text reprefents the perfon, by reafon of whom it was done, as the doer of it himfelf, and fays, "*That he did it in hope.*"

In *hope* of blefling them with a new and better creation.—Thus He, who fat upon the throne, faid, He, would make all things new, notwithftanding his having, at the firft, pronounced them very good.—A manifeft indication, that the original ftate of man was not planned for eternity; was not built for continuance, but to ferve the purpofe of God's love to his Son, and to mankind, as comprehended in him.

He fubjected the creature to vanity, in hope of attaining that glory and honour that had been decreed him, as the Saviour of men: the way to which was through his death on the crofs. But the humiliation of Jefus hath its propriety from a previous fubjection of the creature to vanity, which fenfe (among others) is admitted in our Lord's own words: "*Ought not Chrift to have fuffered thofe things?*"— And again, "*Thus it behoved him to fuffer.*" —Here the fubjection of the creature to vanity is manifeftly pre-fuppofed, and rendered as a reafon of his fufferings and death; yea, and of an obligation that he was under thus to fuffer

and

and die, that he might enter into his glory. This being the hope in which he subjected the creature to vanity, and which hope he perfectly obtained.

Where there is no law there is no transgression.—Without law, man originally could not have sinned: the law therefore entered that the offence might abound. Undoubtedly the first entrance of the law, in substance, was in God's ordinance to *Adam:* " Thou shalt not eat of " it; in the day thou eatest thereof, thou shalt " surely die."—The design of which was not to prevent his fall, nor was it intended as a ministration of life to him, on condition of his obedience, but it entered that the offence might abound; abound to every work, word and thought of every man; abound with judgment and condemnation, to the total reduction of the creature, until every *seeming* avenue of salvation, by man's own obedience, should be shut up from him, and from his posterity for ever.

When lust had conceived, it brought forth sin; the prohibition contained in the law operating on creature curiosity, produced inclination, and stimulated to desire; from the conjunction of the prohibition with this desire (the latter of which is increased by the plainness and positiveness of the former) the offence proceeded, abounding to *Adam* and to all his offspring.

D   But,

But, left it fhould be objected, that this doctrine makes God to act from fovereignty, to the irreparable lofs of his creatures, let it be underftood, that where fin abounded, grace much more abounded; fo that the glory of God, and the eternal welfare of mankind, have been much more promoted by man's death in *Adam*, and his life in Chrift, than they could poffibly have been by his continuance in the ftate wherein he was created.

This revolution being ordained and appointed to ferve the decree of falvation, by the blood of Jefus, is not to be refpected as a matter of accident, a meer fruit of the human will; nor as the produce of fatan's power, cunning, and enmity; but that it was effected by the will of God, a death by him appointed to be the gate of life.

Man being originally formed for the glory of Chrift, and to be an inhabitant in his kingdom, it was not intended that he fhould continue in this world, becaufe the kingdom of Chrift is not of this world.—It is a fond miftake to fuppofe that *Adam*, on condition of his obedience, might have lived for ever in this world; nor is there the leaft fhadow of fuch an implication contained in thofe words; *i. e.* " In the day " that thou eateft thereof thou fhalt furely " die."—Since, as *Adam* lived feveral hundred years after that tranfaction, it is manifeft that

natural

natural death, or that of the body, was not intended in the threatning.

It is indeed faid, that in the midft of the garden, wherein the man was placed, there grew a tree which had life-giving virtues, and of which, if the man had eaten, he might have lived for ever: but this tree, it feems, was not thought of by *Adam* before his fall; and, no fooner was he fallen, than he was driven out from the garden, and his return prevented by the awful cherubim and flaming fword, which turned every way to defend the way of the tree of life, left the man, putting forth his hand, fhould take and eat and live for ever.

This is a myftery, the explication of which I conceive to be as follows: the tree of life was Jefus Chrift: but *Adam*, before his lapfe, being righteous and holy in himfelf, could have no fenfe of the free grace of his God, nor of his everlafting falvation in Jefus: conveniency and neceffity of thefe were not yet known to him, therefore he had no defire to eat. But when none other profpect, than that of the fhadow of death, remained to his view, when fallen a prey to the furies, guilt and defpair, it was revealed to him, that the woman's feed was to be his falvation: then was he difpofed to put forth his hand to take and eat of the tree of life, and ██████ for ever, as implied in the facred text.

Yet,

Yet, as the terms ufed in the promife are literally ambiguous, and rather feemingly import deftruction to the ferpent, than deliverance to man, *Adam* might be naturally enough induced to imagine, that though falvation was intended him, through the woman's feed, or the Lord's Meffiah, it might be conditional, and required the putting forth of the hand, in repentance, contrition, new obedience, &c. in order to his being benefited thereby; and, by thefe means, attempt to re-enter paradife there, by putting forth his hand to take and eat of the tree of life, and live for ever.

When *Mofes* is read, the text fays, " Left " he put forth his hand and take alfo of the " tree of life, and eat and live for ever."— But, when Jefus is read, the text fays, " Who- " foever liveth and believeth in me, fhall never " die."—And again, " He that eateth me, fhall " live by me."—Thus, Jefus is the tree of life which grows in the midft of the paradife of God.

When God drove *Adam* out of *Eden*, it was not with the defign that he fhould never, on any account, eat of the tree of life, or of Chrift, but to prevent in him every fhadow of title to eat thereof, from human merit.— " LEST HE PUT FORTH HIS HAND AND TAKE," faid God; which putting forth of the hand, as it implies a creature act, ▓▓▓▓ with the utmoft metaphorical power made ufe of to diftinguifh

human

human righteoufnefs; for thus we read in the prophet: " If thou take away from the midft " of thee, the yoke, and the putting out of " the finger."—Left *Adam*, by human efforts, or works of righteoufnefs done by himfelf, fhould attempt to eat of the tree of life, or, on the authority of fuch preliminaries, prefume to depend on God's Meffiah for eternal felicity. —I fay, to prevent his afpiring to happinefs by thefe means, God drove out the man from *Eden*, and not only thence, but out from himfelf, alfo from every pleafing hope of falvation, fuggefted by means of felf-fufficiency. And, to keep him under this conviction, to deter him from attempting an entrance by thefe means, God placed before him the cherubim, with the flaming fword, which turned every way to defend the way of the tree of life.

The revelation of God, or the holy fcriptures, are compared to a fword, a two-edged fword; quick, fharp, and powerful, piercing even to the foul and fpirit; and here to a flaming fword, turning every way to keep the way of the tree of life.—The word which God had fpoken to *Adam*, containing a promife of falvation to mankind by the woman's feed, was (in my judgment) the flaming fword, intended in the text. This revelation, or word of promife, being engaged for the glory of Chrift, as the alone Saviour, and to prove and defend his falvation as free, and without works of

righ-

righteoufnefs as done by us, ftands here con-
nccted with the faces of falvation, and waves
as a flaming fword, aweing man from the putting forth of his hand, or from approaching to
eat and live thereby ; *i. e.* from attempting to
attain unto the righteoufnefs of God, by the
eftablifhment of his own righteoufnefs.

However awful and terrible the cherubim
and flaming fword might be to *Adam*'s flefh,
they were yet the gofpel of God to his fpirit,
and defigned to inftruct him in the method of
grace and falvation by Jefus Chrift.—They
taught him, that, by means of Chrift's incarnation, facrifice, refurrection and afcenfion, he
might eat of the tree cf life, and live for ever,
there being none other means of re-entering
paradife, or of his approaching the tree of life
left him but by the cherubim.—Nor was it
poffible for him to come in by them, while he
retained the thought of availing himfelf by the
putting forth of the hand, or by any virtue,
work, or device of his own; becaufe of that
flaming fword, which is ever attendant on the
cherubim; that revelation or word of God,
which maintains that there is none other name,
named in hcaven or on earth, than the name
of Jefus, that contains falvation.

Man, like a thief or a robber, is always
lurking and prying to get in fome other way
than by the cherubim, to plunder the tree of
life, to eat and live : but the word of the Lord,

or

or the flaming fword, ftill prevents him, by turning every way to keep the way of the tree of life.—The word of God ftands armed to oppofe every other way to the tree of life than the cherubimical way, and refolutely and infallibly refifts every human attempt to enter, eat and live, by other means than the cherubim.

We read no more of the cherubim until God commanded *Mofes* to form their likeneffes, as follows : " Thou fhalt make a mercy-feat of " pure gold ; two cubits and a half fhall be " the length thereof, and a cubit and a half " the breadth thereof : and thou make two " cherubims of gold, of beaten work fhalt " thou make them, in the two ends of the " mercy-feat ; one cherub on the one end, " and the other cherub on the other end, even " of the mercy-feat : and the cherubims fhall " ftretch forth their wings on high, covering " the mercy-feat with their wings : and their " faces fhall look one towards another, toward " the mercy-feat fhall the faces of the che- " rubim be, and thou fhalt put the mercy- " feat above upon the ark, and in the ark " thou fhalt put the teftimony which I fhall " give thee."

That the gofpel of falvation, by and *in* Jefus Chrift, was taught in all thefe things, admits of no controverfy.—Firft, the ark itfelf was a figure of Chrift, is manifeft from its ufe, being

a cheft,

a cheft, coffer, or veffel, either to keep in fecrecy, or to preferve from lofs and ruin, fuch valuables as were endearing to the Preferver.—Such was the ark formed for the prefervation of the feeds of the creation in *Noah* and his family, and of the creatures who were with him.—Such was the ark, though made of bulrufhes, or flags, in which *Mofes* himfelf was preferved from the deftruction unto which the *Hebrew* male children were doomed by an *Egyptian* tyrant.—Such was the ark which the fame *Mofes* made according to the pattern fhewn him in the Mount, and which was ordained to contain and preferve the tables of the law, *Aaron*'s rod, and the pot of manna.

The myftery of the rod took its rife from hence: The princes of the congregation, to the number of two hundred and fifty, ftirred up by *Korah* and his affociates, gathered themfelves together againft *Mofes* and *Aaron*; their pretence was, that the brothers took too much authority and fanctity upon them, feeing that the congregation were all holy, and the Lord among them.—Thus tacitly accufing them of lifting themfelves up, from carnal motives, above the congregation of the Lord, they appeared determined to abridge their power.—But this difpofition of theirs brought wrath from the Lord upon them; the earth opened its mouth and fwallowed up *Korah* and his company quick into the pit; and, among the others, a fire

from

from the Lord brake forth, which quickly con-
fumed them. — This occafioned another and
more univerfal murmuring among the people,
which was chaftifed by a plague, whereof died
fourteen thoufand and feven hundred; and, but
for the interpofition of the atonement, they had
been all dead men.

To heal thofe murmurings, and to prevent,
for the future, the heavy chaftifements which
had hitherto followed them, the Lord commanded that the chief of each tribe fhould take
a rod, and that *Mofes* fhould write each perfon's
name upon his rod, and *Aaron*'s name upon the
rod of *Levi*; and that thofe rods fhould be laid
up before the Lord in the Tabernacle of Witnefs; declaring, that the man whom he would
choofe from among them, to minifter in holy
things before him, and to govern the congregation, HE (the Lord) would caufe his rod to
bloffom, that the people by that token (know-
ing the Lord's choice) might have no coloura-
ble excufe for their murmuring.

" And it came to pafs, that, on the morrow,
" *Mofes* went into the Tabernacle of Witnefs,
" and behold the rod of *Aaron*, for the houfe
" of *Levi*, was budded, and brought forth
" buds, and bloomed bloffoms, and yielded
" almonds."—And the Lord commanded that
Aaron's rod fhould be kept for a teftimony
againft the rebels; and that *Mofes*, by this rod,
fhould quite take away their murmuring from

before the Lord.— The rod accordingly was put into the ark.

But there was more intended by this rod than that it fhould be a fign of whom the Lord had chofen to govern his church; it was defigned to take away their murmuring; not by a literal prevention of it through fome phyfical change, for this it did not effect, as appears from their manifold murmurings after this tranfaction.

The rod, in fcripture language, denotes chaftifement: the princes of the congregation were figures of the people, but *Aaron* was a figure of Chrift.— The trial by rods was a revelation of the myftery of the divine will refpecting his choice of a chaftifement for fin, relative both to the object and method.

In brief, *Aaron*'s rod was an emblem of Chrift's fuftaining the chaftifement of our peace. The prophet fays, " The chaftifements of our " peace were laid upon him."—And in the Pfalms we read concerning him : " If his " children forfake my laws, &c. I will vifit " their offences with a rod, &c. neverthelefs, " my loving kindnefs I will not utterly take " from him, nor fuffer my faithfulnefs to fail." --And fo far was the Captain of our Salvation from repining at the rod, or the vifitation of our offences upon himfelf, that the deliverance of mankind was the joy that was fet before him, when he endured the crofs, and defpifed the
shame.—

fhame.—Again, he fays, " Thy rod and thy
" ftaff they comfort me."—And again, " He
" fhall drink of the brook in the way, there-
" fore fhall he lift up his head."—All which
implies, that it was not contrary to his choice
that the judge of *Ifrael* was fmitten on the
cheek with a rod.

The blooming, bloffoming, and fruit of
Aaron's rod, intends the happy confequences
refulting from the fufferings and death of Jefus.
—The forrows and fufferings of Jefus teem
with light, life, and immortality to the fons of
men.—Thefe, cloathed upon with the garment
of falvation, are the fruit of his perfect obedience and bloody toil.—This was the rod which
put away the murmurings of the people from
before God, by expiating the guilt, and blotting
out the remembrance thereof for ever.—Hence,
the figure of this grace and love in *Aaron's*
rod, as a facred depofitum, was placed in the
ark of the covenant, in the tabernacle of witnefs.

The manna alfo, as typical of Jefus, the
bread of life, was preferved in the ark.—When
the *Ifraelites* were fed with manna, in the wil-
dernefs, if they kept it over night it ftank,
became corrupt, and bred worms (the fabbath
excepted): but, when a pot of this manna was
put into the ark, it was preferved in purity for
many generations.—This was defigned to teach
them, that their fpiritual food, and that eternal

E 2   life

life which God had given them, was treasured up in the Messiah, in whom all the treasures of wisdom and of knowledge were hidden, and that it was not in themselves.—Hence, they were not to lay up grounds of comfort and consolation against the morrow, but to have their purity, peace and joy in the Messiah, and therefore always to be found looking unto him as the author and finisher of our faith; while, laying aside every weight, they run the race set before them with patience.

The tables of the testimony were also deposited in the ark, by express command from the Most High: " And thou shalt put into the " ark the testimony which I shall give thee," *Exod.* xxv. 15.—And again; " Take this book " of the law and put it in the side of the ark " of the covenant of the Lord your God, that " it may be there for a witness against thee," *Deut.* xxxi. 26.

A witness! of what? Not on their side, for it was against them: it testified against all their righteousnesses that they were but filthy rags, and that they were altogether incapable of keeping the law contained in the tables : even *Moses* himself, the meekest of the sons of men, had such ungodlike passions, that the tables were not safe in his hands: they could only (in perfection and safety) be kept in Christ, of whom the ark was designed a figure.—In the pierced side of Jesus were the tables to be

depo-

depofited; there was the law to be magnified and made honourable; there to be kept as a witnefs againft all the righteoufneffes of man.

This is further exemplified in the burial of *Mofes*: we are told that God himfelf buried him in a valley overagainft *Beth-peor*; which implies the houfe of the gaping or opening, or the orifice in the fide of Jefus; for certainly here it is that *Mofes* lies buried.

Mofes, and the body of *Mofes*, as terms fometimes ufed in the fcriptures, are to be underftood figuratively, as reprefenting the law given by him.—Thus in the definition which we have in the Epiftle to the *Hebrews*, of the fervant and fon : " *Mofes* as the fervant, faithful " in the houfe of God, who, notwithftanding, " was not to continue in the houfe for ever," certainly intends the law given by him which was to give place to the gofpel, to that grace and truth which came by Jefus Chrift.

Again; the apoftle faith, " *Mofes* hath in " every city them that preach him."—And again, when *Mofes* is read, " The veil is on " their hearts."—Thefe all intend the law which is called *Mofes*, from its being his miniftry; fo, by the body of *Mofes*, we are to underftand the whole of the law in its fulnefs of reafon and fpirit.—This body was buried in the valley of the Lamb's humiliation, having in profpect the blood and water from his pierced fide, and is fpiritually the burial of the body of

Mofes

Mofes in the valley overagainft *Beth-peor*, or the houfe of gaping, or the opening.—God himfelf buried him; nor on the day that the account was written did any man know of his fepulchre.—But in thefe latter days, God fpeaking to us by his Son, has fhewn us that the body of *Mofes* (refpecting the precepts, requifites, and curfes of the law) was buried in the obedience, forrows, and fufferings of Jefus; and therefore the believer in Jefus now knows of the fepulchre of *Mofes.*

We alfo read in *Jude* of *Michael*, the archangel, difputing with the devil about the body of *Mofes*, which I underftand thus: fatan, whofe enmity and rage are ever pointed againft the free falvation of man, by Jefus Chrift, challenged **Michael** to fhew him the fepulchre of *Mofes:* **he contended** that a free falvation was inconfiftent with the law, or body of *Mofes*, arguing, that that body was not yet dead and buried, as no man knew of his fepulchre; *i. e.* that the law had **not** its full and final accomplifhment in the **obedience**, forrows, and fufferings of Jefus, **and therefore** was neither magnified nor made **honourable** by that falvation, fo that the body of *Mofes* had not a juft and honourable burial.—Such was, is, and will be the language of an enemy to the ways of God with man.

But, to return from fuch unneceffary digreffions, as they may probably be thought by fome

who

who may read them, and to draw nearer to the
fubject propofed.—Taking it for granted that
the ark, with its contents, were figurative of
Chrift, his perfon, purity, paffion, and falvation, we have to obferve, that the mercy-feat
was placed over the ark, to fignify that mercy
is built upon Chrift, and on his fulfilling all
righteoufnefs.

From the mercy-feat being made of pure
gold, many ufeful hints might be given, fuch
as of the purity, extenfion, durablenefs, &c. of
divine mercy; but I would, if poffible, avoid
being prolix in the extreme.—The cherubim
being beaten out of one piece of gold with the
the mercy-feat, denotes that the cherubim, or
the faces of falvation, originated from love and
mercy, as properties in the divine nature.—
The cherubim having their faces directed to the
mercy-feat, exhibits a reafon wherefore mercy
fhould be adminiftred thence, wherefore God
fhould in faithfulnefs and juftice forgive man
his fins, and cleanfe him from all unrighteouf-
nefs.

F I N I S.